One of you

A novel based upon the motion picture script
written by Glen Matthew Smith

One of you
Written by Glen Matthew Smith
Copyright © 2017
Copyright © 2022
All rights reserved

Cover media:

Cover:
Copyright © Glen Matthew Smith
One of you productions

Contents

One person commits suicide approx. every 40 seconds.
One person is murdered every 60 seconds.
One person is raped every 60 seconds.

Source:
World Health Organisation
United Nations World Food Program

This is however a novella based upon the events following the novel **'The sharp end of the edge'** by Glen Matthew Smith.

Prologue

She is running. She is scared, hurt, and broken, but she does not stop. She keeps running. The forest fleeting past her is as vivid and surreal as the thought of escape. She has a crawling sense up her spine that there is something behind her, something chasing her, something she just can't shake off. Something dark and cruel with slit eyes upon her at every uncertain twist and turn of the overgrown path through the trees.

She stumbles over something, the hard dirt biting painfully into her face as she careers along the ground. For a moment it all comes back, what she is running from. The death, the pain, and the horror. The cabin. It gets her to her feet and pushes her further through the forest. She does not know how long she can go on, she can barely feel anything, the only thing keeping her going is the adrenalin. Her stride slows, the exhaustion setting in, and her energy drained. But she does not stop, she staggers autonomously on. She thought she would die in that awful cabin.

She comes across a small stream, the meandering beginning of a river, not too difficult to cross, but her weary limbs fault her as she attempts it. She flails in the water, weakly, almost stupidly. For a moment she thinks it is all going to end there, after all this, she will drown in a muddy little stream. Yet, she crawls to the other side, choking the water out, she will not give up. She crawls up through the mud, sliding, and struggling back to her feet. She carries on slowly, every movement forced and painful, but determined to escape.

She does not know when she stopped walking, when the pain became too much. She does not remember when the sun set or when the rain started. It is dark, cold, and lonely. She is too worn out too carry on, too scared not to. She does not remember falling asleep, nor for how long, but when she wakes she is still slumped against a tree. A beaming pearly moon shivering in the sky reveals the clouds and rain have passed. She is shaking from the cold, but she gets up again and carries on. She does not know where she is going, anywhere, anywhere away from that cabin.

She is mumbling incoherently to herself when she finds the dirt road. Who would have thought that an old worn out road could mean so much to somebody, nothing but a sandy track etched away into a beautiful overgrown forest.

Such a simple thing, but for her there and then, it is everything. She almost wants to cry. She is too numb to even sob, she wonders if she is actually crying and just can't feel it any longer, if she is saying things she thought that she was just thinking. She has no shoes on, and as she winds along the gravel road, she does not see her bloody footprints seeping into the sand behind her. She does not notice her body convulsing from the first stages of hypothermia and shock. She should be feeling pain, something, anything. She is wearing only a torn and bloodied shirt, she should be cold, but she feels nothing.

The road is quiet, no destination in the dusky distance, no cars coursing along its forested path. She wishes an angel would come down from heaven and save her, as she did for the past few days, locked up in a cabin with, with them.

She looks around nervously as she walks and picks her pace up again. The little sleep did her good. The rain too, the liquid on her lips has soothed her. She almost feels a slight sense of liberation now, the little path carved out between the trees has given her an ember of hope.

She sobs loudly when she sees the old telephone box. It is a neglected and overgrown, almost consumed by the forest itself, and yet, the sight of it seems to punch the air out of her. It seems so out of place, she almost thinks she is imagining it. She wants to run up to it, to be sure it is real, but her legs feel weak, she has forgotten how tired she is, how far she has run.

She is almost afraid to lift the phone, that if she reaches out she will not feel the weight of the receiver in her hand, that it is just something she is fabricating in her broken mind. And yet, it is real, cold plastic buzzing with a dial tone. Her heart lurches as she dials 999.

'This is the emergency services, what is your emergency?' a voice says into her ear.

She can almost not talk, that wind still escapes from her.

'Hello?' she says softly, her voice quavering and raspy.

'What is your emergency, ma'am?

'They are all dead...' she sobs.

Chapter One

escape

Her name was never printed in the newspaper. But her story was in all of them for weeks. It was not her story per se, it was the story of the washed-out detective who had saved her. A brutal story of how he had died in a cabin in the woods, of how with his last dying breath he had killed his kidnapper. Her kidnapper. It was a story about when they had found that cabin, they had also found the bodies, the girls that did not escape. It was the story of how Jack Sharp had saved her life, and in return had lost his.

Linn was glad that they had made a hero of him, that they had even built a small statue of him in the city. While she was recovering, both mentally and physically, she had tried to read what she could about him, somehow trying to remember a different man than the one scorched into her memory. A memory of Jack hung up like a piece of meat in that dark cabin, being cut up viciously by a murderer called Mervil. She can still smell Mervil's foul breath, his cold sharp scissors against her skin. The memory of that cabin haunts her almost nightly.

Jack was still alive when she finally got free from those bonds. She was a nurse in her previous life, and she was going to save him, she could have saved him, had he not insisted on her looking for something in the cabin first. He was obsessed about it, even with those last few moments of life breathing heavily upon him.

She had found what he wanted, what he knew was there all along. A simple unsuspecting piece of paper with nothing more than a list of names and places on it. It was only then that he finally let her bandage him up as best she could. She could not even find a way to help him down, she had to leave him chained up there before she bolted into the woods for help. It was his last words to her that she will never forget.

'Hey, kid,' he had said as she was opening the door to leave, even trying to feebly smile between his blood-soaked teeth.

'You are one of us now,' he had said, his words icy cold on the morning air, and then she ran.

In a way she feels that she has not stopped running since that day. She did not feel strong enough to go back to work and so she resigned, she had left her apartment in the city and started a new life by the sea.

She had a little stash of savings and would be fine for a few months; fortunately her mother was also not particularly poor, and she could afford the time from work. A rest break by the sea would do her good. Give her a chance to clear her head. The salty sea air would be just the place for that.

She threw away her cigarettes and started running again, and could be seen jogging along the promenade every morning. She loved the sound of the seagulls squawking above the crashing waves. It was very therapeutic, at times she felt it did her more good than the actual therapy.

Yes, her beloved and well-endowed mother insisted that she paid for some expensive slush of a therapist to bore her afternoons with.

What, with everything you have been through, blah blah blah, if you won't talk to me then at least speak to a therapist, blah blah blah.

Mothers can be such cumbersome creatures. She only agreed in order to shut her mother up, especially with what happened to her estranged brother.

To be honest she doesn't really mind the therapy. And if she is quite honest the psychiatrist wasn't really boring, he was even slightly attractive, in a strange thoughtful staring sort of way.

He actually seems to legitimately want to help her. It is a trait that drew her to nursing in the first place, when she was a different person, in a different life. And now here she is, a patient, not even a nurse anymore. Life is strange like that. One day you are on your way to work and then the next you are a victim.

'My name is Linn,' she says to the receptionist.

'I know who you are, Miss Christensen,' the receptionist replies with a hint of sarcasm. Even the way she peers through the spectacles precariously balanced on the end of her long nose makes Linn think the crone could pass for a librarian, or even a schoolteacher. And here is naughty little Linn come to see the headmistress again. *That girl is always in trouble*, is what her mother used to say.

'The doctor is expecting you, please go ahead through to his office.' She waves her hand lazily at the door behind her, and with a sniff continues reading her book.

Linn takes her in again with a grin, trying to imagine what *beak face* here reads, you never can tell with people. She imagines it is something really raunchy, the old girls love that sort of thing. The thought of it turns her grin into a shudder.

The office has so many books it may as well be a library, and hidden away in the corner behind a busy desk buried in more books and patients files is her therapist, clearly enthralled in reading something that looks suspiciously like her file.

She sits down on the sofa and coughs softly.

'Oh, Linn,' he says startled. 'I hadn't noticed you come in.'

'Hey,' she smiles nervously and stretches out

on the sofa. She loves that sofa, it is so soft and comfortable, like a big old teddy bear hugging you. It is clearly the best part of the therapy. A television, some popcorn and this sofa, that's the therapy she really needs.

'You know what I was wondering?'

'What is that, Linn?'

'Have you read all these books?'

'They are mostly reference books, you know that, you were a nurse, weren't you?' He checks the file again. 'A candidate for a doctorate program from the hospital you were formerly employed with. Quite a remarkable opportunity to just throw away.'

Linn sighs; here we go. The one quirk she enjoys about the ever so analytical Dr Williams is his occasional and latent tendency to drift off about his own tangent of problems and take the attention away from her, if even for just a brief moment.

'If I had such a bursary back when I started my studies I wouldn't be earning less than a staff nurse now for the sake of just trying to pay back my student loans,' he says, more to himself.

She doesn't say anything, just curls up on that lush of a sofa and enjoys the few moments of his silent reflection waiting for it to start.

'How are you doing, Linn?'

The circus music begins playing in her head; may as well get the show going.

'I have been having the nightmares again.'

'How often?'

'Every night, almost.'

He sighs.

'Sleepless nights are a common occurrence with patients who suffer anxiety or most commonly post-traumatic stress. A lack of sleep, regardless of the cause, can in itself contribute to exacerbating the condition further. Have you tried the sleeping pills I prescribed?'

'Sleeping causes the dreams, doc.'

He regards her for a moment.

'I would like to try something new with our therapy sessions, Linn, how would you feel about advancing to a more invasive approach?'

'What do you mean?'

'How would you feel about hypnotherapy?'

Bring on the clowns, she thinks.

'Oh, my God, did my mother put you up to this?'

'Now calm down, Linn, from my records your panic attacks have been increasing steadily, clearly the antidepressants are not working either. Let me help you. You are a victim of something that is not your fault, and here you are alone in this city, far away from everybody that loves you.'

'This really is about my mother isn't it? You know, just because she pays you doesn't mean you have to be her bitch.'

Linn gets up to go, she has had enough of Dr Williams for one day.

'Now just you listen here.'

His unusually stern tone stops her dead in her tracks.

'The Linn that walked in here a few months ago couldn't so much as squeak, even if you don't notice it yourself, Linn, you are changing, and it might not be for the better. Some people don't come back from the ordeal you went through. You are lucky somebody in the world actually gives a shit about you.'

She has to sit back down after his outburst. It was so unlike him.

'I am sorry.' He shrinks back a little realising he had lost his usual professional demeanour.

'At least just think about the hypnotherapy sessions, research them a little online. I can wholeheartedly testify that the sessions have helped most of my patients.'

They stare at each other for an awkward eternity.

'That's all I asked you down for today, will I see you on Monday again?'

'Sure, doc.'

'Oh, and one more thing.' He begins scribbling something down, folds the paper and passes it over to her. 'On Sunday evenings I host a group therapy session for victims like yourself. I find that sometimes discussing things with somebody you can relate to...'

'I get it, doc,' she cuts him off, already bolting for the door. 'Good thing I was a nurse,

I would never be able to read it otherwise.'

'I hope you make it down, we start at six,' he says to a closing door.

That night she has the cheapest and strongest bottle of who knows what in her one hand and the whole box of his pills in the other.

Fucking pills, she thinks.

She wants to swallow them all and then down the bottle and just never wake up again. How many times has she pumped the stomach out from lost people like herself so many lifetimes ago, the images of those moments flashing before her eyes.

She never understood back then what drove somebody to it. Back then, when her life was wrapped up in cotton wool and she would scrub her hands at the end of the day with antiseptic soap and be able to forget about it all. There just does not seem to be enough antiseptic soap in the world to wash it away anymore. She throws the pills onto the floor and screams.

Half a bottle later she is staring at her wrists in the bath; she should be feeling better, the alcohol, soap suds, and aroma should be healing her. But she is imagining slitting her cute little wrists and watching the crimson of her life seep down into that beautiful white bubble bath of hers. Again the flashbacks of her patients when she was starting out in an A&E ward. *Why would somebody do this to themselves?* she had asked herself back then.

By the end of the bottle she is out of the bath, still naked and wet, curled up on the dirty tiled floor crying softly to herself. It reminds her of when she was back in the forest, cold, wet, alone and desperate. Sometimes it feels like she will just never escape that place. She just wants it all to end.

Chapter Two

see how she runs

She has been jogging all afternoon, running until she can't run no more, the music of her headphones beating her on, and then further on. It gives her a feeling of flight, as though she can outrun it all, just drift away. As luck would have it she seems to get exhausted right about where that stupid group therapy thing is meant to be. She hadn't even realised she had been running toward it the whole time. She is all sweaty and beside herself when she walks into the little communal hall, clearly interrupting the conversation of the small group of people as she enters.

They are all circled around in those cliché plastic chairs, and her first thought is to turn around and leave. God, they even all have identical stupid paper cups.

Nope, she thinks and turns.

'Linn,' Dr Williams calls out.

Shit. She turns and smiles, a smile that feels all out of place and contorted.

'Hi,' she says awkwardly.

'I didn't think you would make it,' he says beaming a smile as wide as the cheap-ass communal hall in the wrong side of town.

And before she knows it, Linn is one of those

people holding a little paper cup of water, trying her best to get comfortable in a plastic chair, listening to the good doctor's ensemble introduce themselves to her.

The first one calls himself John; he has a thinning hairline that suggests he is reaching middle age, and gives Linn a soft smile.

'My name is Jean,' says the bubbly redhead girl next to him, flashing one of the friendliest smiles Linn has seen in a long while.

'Whatever,' an uninterested and slightly older and dark-haired girl next to her says with almost a yawn. Linn considers the pony-tailed woman and her carved features for a moment.

'Don't worry about Lucy, she is always angry' Jean says with a bemused giggle. Lucy just stares coldly away at a cobweb that suddenly seems more interesting than anything else in the room. Linn's deliberations are broken by a loud snore and her eyes drift to the slumped figure next to Lucy. The sudden sound even gets Lucy's attention, and she roughly shakes the older man awake with her left hand. Linn is surprised by the girl's strength as the big old man is violently torn from his sleep.

'Sorry to wake you, Bill,' the doctor says with a chuckle. 'We have a new member, this is Linn.'

The old guy wipes some spittle from his lips and looks around him, trying to remember where he is.

'Oh, sorry, hello,' he says with a little disorientated wave.

Linn gives a little wave back as a couple of the others try to stifle a giggle.

'So, I guess you all know what happens when we have a new member,' the doctor adds as he digs in a box on the floor. The giggles become a chorus of groans as he starts pulling masks out of the box and handing them out.

They all start reluctantly putting their masks on as the doctor begins explaining.

'We use these therapy masks to break down the walls we build around our psyche,' he says as he hands Linn a mask. 'The physical inhibitions we project to the world around us. The mask makes it easier for us to open those doors, break down those barriers, and be who we really are on the inside. A way for us to express how we really feel without the illusion of our egos holding us back.'

He watches Linn as she awkwardly fits the mask on her face.

'Would you like to start and tell us what you went through, Linn?' he asks.

Linn seems to lose every word she ever knew, as though they all just drained out of her head there and then. She gets an image of that cabin in the woods, a flicker of herself being tied to a table, she feels the sharp scissors against her skin again and recoils, trying to escape the memory.

'Look, maybe this isn't for me,' she says, taking the mask off, dropping it to the floor as though it is going to bite her, and getting up to leave.

'I was raped when I was twelve,' the mask belonging to Jean says. Linn turns and blinks at her.

'He was my cousin, and much older than me, almost a grown man. I screamed and screamed begging him to stop.' Jean's voice breaks a little retelling the story. 'It was so painful, I have nightmares about it, and I can't even be with a partner without it all coming back.'

Linn slowly sits back down.

'Nobody even believed me, it ruined my life.' Jean sobs from behind her mask.

'I was groomed and raped by my teacher,' John's mask says. 'Yeah sure, I bet you thought all rape victims are female, and all rapists are men, my teacher was a woman.'

'I never knew who raped me,' Lucy says, her words as cold as a winter chill blowing from behind her mask. 'I was walking home alone one night, and next thing I knew I was struggling on the ground and being raped, and just like that my life turned into hell.'

'My wife tried to kill me,' Bill says. 'For years she abused me mentally and physically until one day she just tried kill me with my favourite steak knife. I just don't understand it, I was a good husband, never hurt her once in my life. I just don't understand it, why would she do that to me?'

Linn fixes the mask back to her face and tells them everything. She tells them how she had finished her shift at the hospital, was getting into her car, and then everything went black. How she woke up in a rundown cabin in the woods naked and tied spreadeagled to a table. She painfully recalls that twisted face with scissors that torments her. Then she tells them about the private detective named Jack who had saved her, and lost his life for it. She tells them how she had to watch them both die, how she struggled to eventually break free and then ran through the woods for days. She does not even notice she is crying when she stops recalling the events.

Dr. Williams wraps an arm warmly around her, gently takes her mask off and gives her a few tissues.

'Well done, Linn,' he says softly, and purses his lips proudly at her.

When she looks back up, everybody else has their masks off too, and she can see that their eyes are all just as red and wet as hers.

And for the first time in a long while she doesn't feel completely alone and isolated. Jean walks over and gives her a big hug, and Linn squeezes her back tightly. God, she needs a hug right now, so damn much.

'I read about that in the newspapers,' John

says.

'That Jack, he was always in the newspapers.' Bill says thoughtfully and nodding slowly. 'Last I heard he blew up the harbour and half the cartel with it.'

'Right,' the doctor says, digging in his box again like some macabre two-bit magician looking for his next trick. 'As you know, every week I try to suggest something to help you guys when you are all feeling a bit down.' He gives a toothy grin and pulls out a stack of newspapers. 'This is one of my favourites.'

The formidable Dr Williams stands while rolling up one of the newspapers and slides an empty chair into the middle of the circle.

'This is a stress relief exercise that you can do if you ever feel angry, or just want to get some bad energy out of you. It is a tried and proven technique,' he says, tapping the rolled up paper in his hands as though it is a weapon.

'All you have to do is roll up a newspaper nice and tight and then focus on all that darkness in you, all that bitterness, everything that is making you angry.' He stops and reflects for a moment. 'For me it is my wife trying to divorce me,' he says with a sudden malevolence, and slams that rolled up baton of paper hard down on the chair.

Thwap!

The sound reverberates loudly around the

room.

'Just focus on all that negative energy and get it out of you,' he says. 'Like lawyers.'

Thwap!

Thwap!

'Fluffing flocking lawyers,' he says louder and a little more vehemently.

Thwap!

Thwap!

Thwap!

'Just let it all go,' he says wiping a little sweat off his brow with his shoulder.

This time he does not stop, he just keeps hitting that chair muttering things about accountants, lawyers and estate agents. It seems even the doctor himself has some pent up shit to deal with.

'For God's sake,' Lucy sneers, promptly turns, and walks out.

Linn and Jean watch her light a cigarette and stare into the growing darkness of night outside the ajar door. Jean smiles and shrugs at Linn and they both look back at the doctor.

'Can I try?' John asks coyly, but it seems the good doctor doesn't even hear him.

'These patients are all driving me slowly mad,' the doctor now shouts, and starts hitting down again.

Thwap! Thwap! Thwap!

While Jean starts grabbing newspapers from the pile for the rest of the group Linn decides to sneak out too. She joins Lucy by the door, a little surprised it has started raining, Lucy does not even seem to care.

'Don't you wish you could have killed him yourself?' Lucy says, staring out at the rain.

'What?' The sudden question takes Linn a little aback.

'I mean,' she says, sparking a cigarette butt into the street. 'Really got your own hands around that a-hole's neck and killed him yourself, instead of watching Jack do it?'

'I don't,' Linn stammers. 'I don't know.'

'You see,' Lucy says looking down at Linn – she is taller than Linn and towers a little over her – 'unlike that lot, I don't fight plastic chairs.' She pokes her thumb toward the room and they both look back to watch the group taking their anger out on newspapers and their chairs.

'I have learned how to fight back,' Lucy says and shoves a fist into Linn's chest. Linn looks down and sees Lucy's hand holding a business card.

'Martial arts,' Lucy says when Linn carefully takes the card from her clenched fist. 'You should come try it.' Lucy winks at her and walks off. Linn watches her get on a motorbike, put a helmet over her head, rev the bike up and drive off before she looks down at the card.

Learn self-defence

Is all it says, and she turns it over and there is an address on the other side. Linn looks back at the meeting and decides to make her own silent escape, listening to the *thwap thwap* sounds fade away into the rain and approaching night behind her.

Chapter Three

three is a crowd

It was a good night for the two sisters, a good club, good music, a good weekend for them to let their hair down. The club was bumping, the drinks flowing, and the boys taking notice of them. It was perfect until Ria, the younger of the two, decided to start hurling her guts out into the piss-stained porcelain lavatory. The whole thing was starting to bring Clio down; it was meant to be a good night out, they didn't often get time together anymore.

'And they say you are the pretty one, if only they could see you now,' Clio says, watching a wasted Ria wash her face in the sink. The running mascara down her face paints an eerie mask over her younger sister's face.

'I really don't feel well, I think there was something in my drink,' Ria says weakly.

'And here I thought you were doing all this to stay skinny like the self-conscious little drama queen you are.'

Ria does not even get a chance to answer before she starts another round of throaty chorus right there into the sink.

'Why do you always have to be such a bitch?' she finally spits out weakly. 'I am serious, I feel like shit.'

Clio tenderly holds Ria's long hair out of the sink.

'Because I am your sister and I care about you. God, let's just go home,' Clio decides. It is so typical of her sister to just ruin everything, as always.

She dries her sister's face as best she can with tissues and the two of them slowly saunter their way down the club stairs onto the street.

They decide to catch the cool evening breeze and enjoy a sobering walk home rather than a taxi; their parents would kill them both if Ria rocked up looking like a crack addict. Clio knows she would get the brunt of it, being the older sister, they barely even had much to drink.

As they make it down a few blocks Ria just gets worse, and it is not long before Clio is propping her up and contemplating calling that taxi after all. As she fumbles with her handbag to get her mobile phone out, she does not notice the shady figure sliding slowly in behind them. It is when Ria just falls down, completely out for the count, that everything turns from bad to worse. Her sister drops down on one side, and her phone out of her other hand. She is still deciding which to pick up first when the shadowy shape behind hits her hard on her head and the night gets a whole lot darker.

Clio wakes up with the world around her shaking and rattling, the back of her head stirring with thick pulses of pain. She probably passes out, overcome with it once or twice until her eyes get accustomed to the darkness and she realises she is lying in the back of what must be some sort of van. She can't see her own hands in front of her and her head stings brutally but she forces herself up and fumbles around the darkness until she finds what feels like skin, a leg, and then an arm. She blindly feels her sister's face and breathes a desperate sigh of relief when Ria starts groaning softly and incoherently. Then, with a sudden impulse of horror she starts frantically shaking her sister awake, screaming with terror.

The van stops suddenly, nothing more than the muffled sounds of traffic outside, then she can hear the music in the van get turned on full blast before it starts driving again. It must all just be a bad dream, a nightmare, she keeps telling herself, as she tries to wake her sister up. Ria does little more than feebly push her away as though she is having a good old dream and does not want to be disturbed. Clio screams and bangs on the sides of the van, but the music is too loud, drowning her efforts out; she feels around and finds the door latch but it is locked from the other side. In the end she can do little else but resign herself to holding her sister in her arms, sob to herself in the darkness, and listen to the van rattle along to God knows where.

When the van does finally stop, the sound of the traffic is long gone, and they have gone a long way down what must be a bumpy road in what she is guessing to be the countryside. Ria is still comatose, and she can feel her own heart beating faster as the sound of a car door closing turns into the scratching of footsteps on gravel working their way to the back of the van. She has never been so terrified in her life before, but as she hears somebody beginning to work the lock of that back door she gets a sudden surge of adrenalin coursing through her, a mad rage boiling in her like a wild animal. As the first crack of light reveals itself, she bursts through the door, clawing desperately at the surprised silhouette in the doorway. She is thrown aggressively to the ground, the force knocking the wind right out of her. She can all but watch a boot stamp down hard on her face and then a rain of painful punches leaning into her until she succumbs to the darkness again.

Chapter Four

psycho

'I want you to concentrate on the sound of my voice.'

Linn closes her eyes.

There is still the sound of ticking somewhere in the background. Gently coming and going, coming and going. Was it a clock? He had pulled a pocket watch out, that was it. Asked her to listen to it, watched it swing around in his hands. Around and around. She feels so....

'You are feeling sleepy,' the voice says somewhere in the distance.

'So sleepy,' she says softly.

'Tell me what you are dreaming about,' the voice says soothingly.

'I am walking through mud.'

'Where are you walking to?'

'I don't know.'

'What do you see now?'

'There is a door.'

'What is behind the door?'

'I don't know.'

'Do you want to open the door?'

'I am scared.'

'I want you to open the door.'

'I don't want to.'

'Linn, open the door.'

'My hands are shaking.'

'Open the door, Linn.'

She opens the door.

'What do you see?'

'I see myself.' She sounds horrified.

'I am tied up.'

'I have been hurt.'

'Wait, there is something wrong.'

'What is wrong?'

'It is not me. I shouldn't be here.'

'What is wrong, Linn?'

'I am running away.'

'Where are you now?'

'I am in the forest,' Linn sobs.

'Are you running away from the cabin?

'Yes,' she says weakly, almost as though she is there again, the horror of it all only moments ago. She can smell pine in the air, a cold shiver on her skin.

'Do you remember anything you forgot about that day, that you haven't told me?'

He is grasping at straws at the moment, but if he can just...

'There is a list,' she says.

'A list of what, Linn?'

'Them.'

'Who?'

'I was trying to save him,' she sobs.

'The detective?'

'There was so much blood,' she sniffs tearfully and the thick metallic smell of blood overcomes her. She looks down at her blood-soaked hands and the haunting figure hanging helplessly before her.

'He said there is more of them.'

'More of who, Linn? People like the man that abducted you?'

'I can't make the bleeding stop,' Linn cries.

'Please just make it stop.' She is almost hysterical now.

'You are fine, Linn, you are just dreaming. Listen to the sound of my voice. Pay attention to my words. You are just dreaming, and in a few seconds you are going to wake up in my office. You are safe, Linn. You are calm and relaxed. You were just sleeping, and now you are awake.' He snaps his fingers loud enough to stir her awake.

Linn sits bolt upright and glares at her therapist. She vaguely remembers agreeing to a hypnosis session. She remembers laughing and saying it would never work on her.

'What did you do?'

'Relax, Linn, you were only asleep, as I said before, it is called lucid dreaming, how do you feel?'

Fuck my mother, and your fucking therapy, that's how I feel, she thinks to herself.

'Linn, sometimes dreams are just a way for our mind to process things. They often feel real, but you are not in any danger anymore. You have nothing to be scared of. You are safe now, you escaped, Linn, you are one of the lucky ones.'

'One of the lucky ones?' She can barely get the words out of her mouth. 'Then tell me, doctor, why I don't feel so lucky?'

Linn does not know why she is so angry, but she slams the door behind her and leaves that therapy session with a thunder of rage and frustration boiling in her. A headache as though there are bugs crawling around inside her brain. She hates those nightmares, and she hates that damn therapist prodding around in her head. She feels like she just wants to punch something, hell, at that moment she would tear a leather ball apart with her teeth like a rabid dog if she could.

That is how Linn finds herself steaming down the promenade, sprinting more than jogging, trying to run that feeling off her, as though she can shake it off her tail, outrun it all. She is never going to lose those nightmares, the sudden attacks of terror, that empty feeling inside of her. She does not think she can even be intimate with anybody ever again.

Her face is so soaked with salty tears and sweat, her mind so clouded that she barely even notices the figure almost shouting her name. She slows down and loops back to find a grinning Lucy on the promenade green.

Lucy gives a heavily breathing Linn a few minutes to get her air back. The girl is almost choking. Lucy can even see Linn's legs slightly shaking from the exertion.

'It's me, Lucy, from therapy, you remember, crazy Lucy.'

Linn tries to chuckle but starts coughing, and instead just nods her head between gasps.

'I have never seen anybody run that fast in my life before,' Lucy chuckles. 'Girl, you looked like a naughty kid running from her mother's slipper.'

They both giggle it off, Linn feeling a little embarrassed, and sensing it Lucy points behind her.

'Look, this is what I was telling you about,' she says.

Behind Lucy are a mixed bag of about ten people all dressed for the gym doing various fighting exercises and martial arts exhibitions. It is all quite impressive and somewhat daunting to her.

'We come down here occasionally to promote the dojo.' Lucy considers Linn for a moment. 'There is somebody I want you to meet.'

Before Linn has a chance to protest, because she really isn't in the 'making new friends' mood, Lucy has already motioned somebody over.

'Linn, this is our Sifu,' Lucy says proudly as a middle-aged man approaches them. He has a strong build, not overly muscular, just a good stocky strength to him. Quite ordinary looking otherwise.

'It means teacher,' he smiles at her and gives a small nod that is almost a hint of a bow.

'This is Linn, she said she's interested in joining the dojo.'

'I did?'

It was more of a question but the *Sifu* breaks out with a gleaming hopeful smile that Linn doesn't have the heart to shatter.

'That's great news, wonderful, here take one of our pamphlets,' he says and proudly hands Linn a glossy fold of paper.

'You are going to love it.' Lucy gives a big cheesy grin almost rivalling that of her teacher. 'It's better than hitting chairs with newspapers like a bunch of loonies,' she adds, and both are giggling together again like two shameful little girls.

Linn makes her excuses and after a few polite smiles and goodbyes she is jogging along the beach again, feeling a little more relaxed, enjoying the day a little more. She ends the afternoon cooling down on the edge of the water watching a blissful sunset, and finding herself reading the dojo's pamphlet over and over.

Learn to fight back, it says.

Chapter Five

sisters of sufferance

Clio has never felt so awful in her life, but she tears herself out of the darkness, towards the pain, always crawling closer and closer towards the light and the pain. *Oh dear God, the pain*. The closer she seems to edge towards it the more intense and brutal it becomes. Part of her just wants to crawl back into the darkness but she can hear herself saying her sister's name over and over again. Ria is in trouble. She has to push through the pain.

It hurts everywhere as the light hits her with a dark horrible sense of awareness. *Oh God, the pain*. She can feel her face just isn't right, her lips all swollen, everything puffed up, her one eye so battered she can barely see out of it. Her mind trying to piece things together. Her body feels broken.

'Ria...' she manages to wheeze out of her lips.

'Ria,' she says a little more urgently as the foggy cloud begins to thin.

'Ria!' she almost wails as she gropes blindly at the darkness around her.

She seems to be in a barn or something, the ground covered in hay. If only she could breathe properly, she sobs a thick wet sound out in despair.

'I am here,' a fractured voice says out of the

darkness.

Clio scrambles desperately towards her sister and the two clutch at each other until they are holding one another in their arms, neither of them ever having squeezed or held each other so tightly before, neither of them wishing to let go. Both of them ice cold and yet shaking more in fear.

'Where are we, Clio?'

'I don't know, little sis. Don't worry, I will look after you, I promise.'

They hold on to each other until they can begin to see the edges of light slowly begin to slither between the cracks of the wooden walls around them. They are still clutching at each other when the footsteps outside approach. The door of their small wooden stall opens and he comes in holding something in his hand. The figure is obscured by the intense light of the ajar door in the dark little room.

'Do you know what this is?' he asks, a sadistic tone to his voice.

'It is a cattle prod,' he answers himself. 'And it hurts like a son of a bitch.' He gives a malevolent chuckle as his gaze seers down onto them. 'I made some adjustments of my own to it,' he snickers and stabs it down at Clio. 'For all the naughty girls who do not want to listen,' he laughs as the electric prod sends thousands of volts into her.

The pain jolts her backwards and she crashes

involuntarily into the corner in time to watch that bastard dragging Ria out of the room. Her tiny sister screams in horror, unable to overpower him. Clio recovers herself and pounces at him, but she is met with that awful pain as the electricity forces her back again, and she gets a few kicks from him for good measure, the door slams closed and then she is alone.

Clio struggles with agony but manages to crawl towards the door and see small snippets between the wooden panels. Sometimes craning an ear to the cracks to hear what was being said, sometimes an eye to see.

'Take your clothes off.'

'I don't want to,' Ria cries, her voice trembling. 'Why are you doing this?' she pleads.

Clio can't see her sister, but she can see him. He is setting a camera onto a tripod. Once he is finished he sighs, grabs his prod again, and walks out of view. A moment later she can hear Ria screaming her lungs out. Clio can't help but bang on the door and scream herself.

The door flies open and a pair of hands drags her out into a barn.

'Look at your sister!' he howls.

She can see Ria getting up off the floor, a terrified look on her face, before she feels the familiar sting of electricity coursing through her again.

'Oh, sis,' Ria sobs, welling up at seeing her

bruised, swollen and bloody sister on the ground. 'Oh, Jesus.'

'Just do as I say, and I won't hurt you,' is all Clio hears before he punches her and the lights go out again. For a moment she can almost hear the birds singing somewhere in the distance before the sweet numbness of sleep takes her into its welcoming arms.

When Clio once again stirs herself out of the deep mist, the little room is back in darkness. A whole day gone already. The sickening sense of pain stretches its dark claws even deeper into her than before. Stifling her like a thick wet and blood-soaked blanket. She can barely speak and manages to just grunt and then cough up some blood. She dry heaves but there is nothing in her left to come out. She can feel her jeans are damp, she must have soiled herself, and the strange thing is she is too beat up and terrified to even care. The only thing she can think of is her little sister, and once again she begins to painfully flounder in the darkness looking for her.

'It's okay, big sis, I am here,' a voice says out the darkness, a beautiful gentle voice that she loves so much. She can feel a soft warm arm wrap around her and pull her tightly into an embrace.

'Are you...?' Clio sobs, almost in tears. Her words almost muffled in her swollen mouth. She is almost sure some of her teeth are broken. Her tongue feels as though it is exploring somewhere alien, something wretched, not her own mouth.

'I am fine,' Ria consoles her, pausing a few moments before continuing.

'He says you have to stop fighting him, sis.'

Clio shivers, and starts crying at the memory of the violence she's suffered.

'I was trying to,' she says, her mouth trying to form the words in her new broken mouth. 'To protect you.'

'I know, sis, I know. Don't worry nothing happened.'

Clio sobs through her clogged nose hearing the words, all the awful possibilities running around her head. Her eyes are all puffed and welled with tears, she can't see more than slight shapes and shadows.

'He just took some photos of me,' Ria tries to reassure her.

'I promised to protect you, I failed you,' Clio wails uncontrollably.

'Shhh, it's okay.' Ria tries to console her older sister as though she were a babe in her arms. 'He hasn't hurt me, yet.' It was supposed to make her feel better but the words hang in the air like the scent of a bad omen.

'He gave us some food, please try to eat something, sis.'

Clio tries to eat, but her mouth has grown

stubborn, chewing too painful, her jaw struggling to open or close. In the end Clio just gives up and allows Ria to pour a little water into her mouth from a plastic bottle. Ria is even considering chewing some food for her sister but can already hear the feverish snoring. So instead she tears a small seam from her dress and soaks the small cloth in the last remaining water and tries to gently clean her sister's dirty and battered face. She can't remember when she started whimpering and she doesn't stop until her own eyes grow heavy and sleep takes her. Somehow, the farm sounds and countryside in the background help ease her a little, if even for just a short while.

Chapter Six

Nugget

Linn has already been down to the dojo several times in the past couple of weeks, and Lucy was right, it sure beats running herself ragged along the beach every day. Tearing herself apart from the inside out. She still loves her jogging but now she feels like she has more of a balance in life. Learning how to take her aggression out on the punch bags has been a great help, and she smiles as she recalls having to learn how to punch first.

'I am learning self-defence now,' she says proudly. 'You would like it, I think, it's some sort of old martial art.'

Linn isn't talking to anybody in particular, there is nobody but a field full of graves around her. But she is somewhat talking to one grave in particular. She had found the detective's, Jack's, grave not long after she got out of therapy, or as her mother liked to call it, a wellness clinic, whatever the hell that meant. She will occasionally catch a bus out here and spend a couple of hours trying to get things off her chest. It is easier than talking to a damned therapist. Even oddly handsome ones like the formidable Doctor Williams that her mother had picked for her.

'I still don't speak to my mother much,' she

says. 'I know I should make more of an effort, I just find it so difficult to speak to people anymore, and even then it's only because I have to,' she sighs and stares at a grave that says *Jack Sharp*.

She watches an odd little shape work its way slowly up the path that cuts through the graveyard. It seems to hobble a little more than walk, and as it nears she can begin to clearly see it is a slightly portly man with glasses carrying a small bag. She watches him slowly amble his way up the path and then turn towards her. She can only stare as he walks up to her, not paying her any attention and sits down on the grass right there beside her.

'Hi, Jack. Hi, Linn,' the figure says as he begins to empty out the contents of his bag and lay them out meticulously in front of him.

He is going to have a picnic right here, Linn thinks to herself and can't help but gawk at him.

'I am sorry, do I know you?' She blinks in disbelief, or maybe there is something in her eye, and she rubs it a little trying to hide the fact she has been crying.

'You are Linn Christensen, I read about you in the newspaper. Jack saved you,' he smiles up at her, for the first time facing her.

'Jack is my best friend,' he says, beaming a bigger smile, and then focuses his attention back to organising his lunch neatly. He opens a small plastic box and starts munching down on a sandwich.

'And what's your name?' Linn says as affably as possible; having worked as a nurse it hasn't taken her long to realise that Jack's friend here most likely suffers a neurologic disorder, probably similar to a low level autism.

'Oh, I am Nugget.' He pokes a thumb at himself and takes another bite of his sandwich.

'Nice to meet you, Nugget,' she smiles, but he doesn't seem to take any more notice of her.

'I used to eat my lunch in the park,' he says looking into the distance. 'But now I eat it here with Jack.' He then looks back at her and smiles.

'Jack was a detective.'

'He was a very good detective,' Linn agrees, wiping another little tear out of her eye.

'I used to help him, he said I am very special,' Nugget says while chewing on his second sandwich.

'I bet you were a great team.'

'It is because I have a good memory,' he says nonchalantly.

Linn thinks a short while as they are both sitting there in silence, and then fumbles around in her bag.

'Before he died, Jack asked me to look for this,' she says cautiously as she pulls out the list of names she found in the cabin.

Nugget perks his eyes at her like a big old puppy, a wry grin rippling across his face.

'Are you also working on Jack's case?' he says with a boyish enthusiasm.

'Did Jack ever tell you about a list of names? It is what Jack asked me to find.' She hesitates and then gives him the slip of paper.

Nugget looks at the names for a short while, and flips the paper over expecting more, disappointment growing on his face on finding it blank. He then loses interest and looks at the fresh flowers on the grave.

'Do you bring the flowers? They are pretty. I like it when you bring Jack flowers, nobody else does,' he says, forgetting about the list of names altogether.

'He said they are people like Mervil,' Linn presses on.

At the mention of the name of the man that killed Jack, Nugget shudders, almost throws the piece of paper back at her, and begins packing his lunch back up hastily.

'Mother says I have to be back early today,' Nugget says as he stands.

'Bye, Jack,' he says as he waves at the grave and then gives her a long dark stare.

'Be careful of them, Linn Christensen, they are not nice people,' is all he says before he turns and leaves her sitting there alone in a graveyard again, feeling as if a cold shadow has just passed over her own grave.

Chapter Seven

victims

'You aren't angry enough.'

'God damn it, I am trying my best here.'
Linn is exhausted but she presses on.

'Come on, Linn, imagine I am him, imagine
I am your kidnapper.'

Linn throws a punch forward as hard as she
can. Lucy takes a deft sidestep and the clumsy
swing misses her. She rewards Linn with an easy
jab that slaps a padded hand square across her
face.

'If you don't get angry you will always be a
victim. Is that what you want, Linn? To be a
victim all your miserable little life?'

Lucy watches a red-faced Linn scream and
try to throw another punch at her, just as
clumsy as the first. So Lucy rewards her with a
mighty slap with her left pad. The swing catches
Linn off balance and crashes her hard down
onto the mat. Lucy is stronger than her by a
mile, and a brilliant fighter, a fact Linn is now
painfully beginning to learn. She aches there on
that boxing ring floor. She looks down and
watches the blood pouring out of her nose onto
the mat.

'Or are you a quitter, Linn?' Lucy sneers
down at her.

Lucy has taken Linn under her wing at the dojo, being an instructor there herself, and the two of them have done nothing but train for hours every other day. Linn feels herself getting stronger, her body ripping its muscles tighter, muscles she didn't even know she had.

Lucy is a monster in a fight, she even gives most of the male contingency of the dojo a good seeing to. She is a merciless instructor, and a complete bitch at times, if Linn is completely honest. But she knows deep inside Lucy is just needling them, trying to make them all better fighters.

She tries to get up but her arms are too weak, she just crashes back down onto the mat, spent; she rolls over and awkwardly tries to stop her nose bleeding with a gloved hand.

Lucy looks down at her and sighs in disgust.

'What if I told you, I know where more of them are?' She doesn't know why she even said it, she hadn't planned to.

'More what? Victims and quitters? I see enough of them every Sunday at our good therapist's freak show, thanks for the offer though.' Lucy starts taking the pads off her hands in resignation.

'Stop being a bitch, Lucy. I think I know where more kidnappers are.'

Lucy looks down at Linn; she isn't doing a good job of pinching her nose with a boxing glove on. The blood is still seeping into her mouth make her words all thick, wet, and gushy.

'You must be concussed. Damn, girl, I didn't even smack you that hard,' Lucy says, leaning down over her, a slight sound of amusement in her voice.

She throws the gloves down, helps Linn take hers off, and figuring training is over for the day she walks herself into the showers. A few minutes under the hot water and she will be Lucy again. The bit between her teeth is still there, just a little softer to the touch. She hated being a victim, being raped had made her a good fighter, it made her angry, bitter and twisted, but she will make damn sure she will never be a victim again, or a quitter.

Linn eventually joins her in the showers and after a little time under the steamy water, a little shampoo in their hair, they are all relaxed again. It is only while they are dressing that Lucy remembers what Linn has said. It was the oddest thing.

'What do you mean, you know where more kidnappers are?'

Linn sighs; she wish she hadn't said a word now. So she explains about Jack still busy being a detective while he is even bleeding to death, sending her on a wild goose chase around the cabin looking for clues.

'I think Jack had some sort of hunch there

was more than just one person involved in whatever *he* was doing.'

She can't even say Mervil's name. Even the thought of him, talking about him, is making her feel nauseous.

Lucy stares at her thoughtfully.

'Let me get this all straight,' she starts slowly, trying to figure it all out for herself. 'You got kidnapped, almost raped, had it not been for a detective that magically shows up. Detective gets himself kidnapped, and then killed by said kidnapper but not without killing the kidnapper himself first. While detective and kidnapper are both busy bleeding to death, you break free, and being a nurse you try save the detective.'

Linn nods slowly in agreement.

'So our good detective then gets you to start digging around the cabin because he has a nasty suspicion that the kidnapper is part of some sort of collective that abducts girls?'

Linn nods. 'I found a list of names.'

Lucy pauses while she mulls it over.

'What do they do with the girls they abduct?' Lucy asks, more to herself than anything.

'I don't bloody know, they all bloody died, didn't they?' Linn is standing up and the growing tears are starting to make her eyes swim in two little pools.

Lucy stands, grabs her friend tight, and comforts her with the biggest bear hug she can.

'Come on then, first beer is on me.' Lucy

smiles down at her.

'Bitch,' Linn chuckles out at her.

'Don't forget it, girlfriend,' Lucy replies and they both have a well-earned giggle together, just two naughty little girls again.

A short drive later the two of them are chugging the bottles down in some crappy rundown place with a jukebox and cheap beer. The kind of place you buy your beer in bottles because you know the glasses aren't clean. A few of the happy-go-lucky boys come over and try to chat the two of them up, but after Lucy growls at them, the little alpha males back away with their tails between their legs and give the two of them all the peace and quiet they need.

'At least the beer is cold here,' Lucy says, downing her third bottle of beer. 'One thing still bugs me though.'

'The flies?' Linn says, waving a bar fly away from her face.

'No, with your story, silly,' Lucy grins and cracks another beer open. 'Why didn't you tell the cops about this list?'

Now it is Linn's turn to slowly down a beer while she thinks.

'I don't know, I wanted to, I tried to. But I figured they probably didn't believe Jack, why would they believe me? I mean hey, he was a cop too.'

A grin rips across Lucy's face.

'I knew there was a fighter in you,' Lucy circles her finger around at Linn. 'Hiding away in there behind that little casualty you have become.'

'Oh yeah? How do you figure that?'

'Well,' Lucy starts and downs another beer before she continues. 'You said there are places next to those names, didn't you?'

'Yeah?'

'Well, you and I are going to find them,' Lucy says, sounding a little drunk.

She slams the lid off another couple of beers. 'But first, friend, we are going to get drunk and then we are going to go dance until we can dance no more.'

They seal the agreement by slamming their beers together and proceeding to do that very thing. They find a good club where the music is somewhat bearable, and lost in the sway of dance, cheap booze, and drunken drum beats they proceed to forget, if only for a few short hours.

The sun is teasing the horizon again when they find themselves watching it slowly rise on the beach. The two of them are quietly listening to the *swoosh swoosh* sounds of the waves as the tide begins to slowly ebb back out to sea.

'I really had fun tonight, thank you.' Linn breaks the silence.

'It's morning, silly.'

'I know, I just wanted to thank you, for everything.'

Lucy stops leaning against Linn and stares her deadpan in the eyes before giving her a big fat wet kiss right on the smacker.

'I am serious, you know.'

'Serious about what?' Linn says absentmindedly lost in the moment; *did Lucy just kiss her?*

'About finding out about that list.'

'And how you figure to do that?' Linn suddenly feels very drunk. Or is it just the earth spinning? You don't normally feel the earth spinning, do you?

'By finding the first name on that list,' Lucy says and stands up. She dusts the sand off herself and offers her hand to help Linn up.

'Or do you still want to be a victim?'

Linn stares at Lucy's hand.

Swoosh, says the sea.

GLEN MATTHEW SMITH

Chapter Eight

ghosts

Linn is at her apartment packing when the doorbell rings. She begins to unlatch the door subconsciously but stops herself.

'Who is it?' she asks nervously as she is startled by another series of loud rings.

'It's Dirk,' a voice says from the other side of the door, a voice that turns Linn ice cold, a name she has almost forgotten.

When she opens the door, there is a stranger standing in front of her, not her long-lost brother barely out of his teens.

'Surprise,' he says.

A few strong coffees later, and they are staring at each other from across a dusty table in her dimly lit kitchen.

'So Mother finally found you? How many years has it been since you left us?'

'Yeah, I was in Thailand just doing my own thing on an island and some guy walks up to me, hands me a phone, and on the other side is our mother.'

'Eighteen years, Dirk, eighteen years she has been looking for you,' she answers her own question. 'She never gave up once.'

'Our mother is a persistent one, that is for

sure.'

'Why did you run away?'

'I didn't *run away*,' he jibes back at her. 'I was almost twenty years old, and after Pa died, I just, I just didn't feel like it was home anymore.'

'You broke her heart, and the not knowing almost killed her, day after day, year after year.' She studies his face, trying to find the brother she used to look up to and admire.

'I am sorry, Linn. I should have called. I know that now. I wanted to.'

Linn sneers, not believing a word of it.

'The longer I left it, the harder it became.'

He tries to meet her eyes but she looks away.

'Then about a month ago, after my wife died, I got really drunk, and for a moment I just missed Pa, and having a family, so I tried to call home. I hung up after Mother answered. I think she knew it was me, because a few days later she found me.'

'I am sorry about your wife, I didn't even know… I mean, how could we?' Linn sighs.

'She is worried about you, Linn.'

'So you are just going to come swooping in after being gone for more than half my life, and play pretend happy families now?'

'You don't answer her calls, Linn. Why don't you just talk to her?'

'Of all people, I think you are the worst person to come lecturing me. In fact why don't you just leave.' She stands up and pours a cold cup of coffee into the sink.

'Fine, Linn, you are right,' he says as he lifts his hands into the air in surrender. 'You know what, I promised her I would come talk to you, and I tried.' He gets up to leave, he knows it will take time, it is a lot to take in for one morning.

'Tell *Mother* I am going out of town for a while, I will call her when I am back,' is all she says as she slams the door behind him.

She punches the door in frustration after she hears him walking away. She stands back and admires the hole she made. A month ago she wouldn't have even been able to punch that hard, a month ago she would have broken her hand trying.

When she gets downstairs Lucy is already waiting for her. They decide to take her car and load the back up with a few suitcases then, with a deep breath, Linn starts the engine.

'I guess we are really going to do it then?' she asks as the car starts rolling forward.

'Hell yeah, we are going on a road trip,' Lucy yells excitedly.

Linn shoves the car into second gear, laughs out loud and thumbs the car stereo up to 11.

'Rooooooaaaaaad ttttrrrrriiiiiiiiiipppppp,' the two of them cheer in unison as the car drifts down onto a highway. Nothing but a whole lot of open road in front of them.

On the other side of town four people sit in an empty communal hall staring at each other while drinking water from little paper cups. They shift uncomfortably around in their plastic chairs, waiting. A heavy sense of impatience growing in the air.

'So does anybody know where Lucy and Linn are?'

Silence.

Williams sighs and looks down at his watch for the hundredth time.

'Look, if we aren't going to do this group therapy, I have other places I can be. You know, like go out, make some friends, as you are always telling me to do. I like you guys and all but I really don't want to be here if I don't have to,' Jean says, a little unlike herself, but they are all getting a wee bit irritable after an hour of waiting.

Williams holds a finger to one ear and his phone to the other as his call is connected.

Ring ring.

Ring ring.

'Hello, this is Linn, sorry I can't take your call right now...'

'Linn, this is Doctor Williams, we are all down at group session and you aren't here, Are you with Lucy? Can you call me, please?'

He hangs up and sighs. He is still sitting there as he watches Jean, Bill and John all get up and leave him alone with nothing but his thoughts to echo around in that big old room.

Chapter Nine

a road trip

Lucy is studying Linn's list. It's a little difficult to read but she can make out most of the names. Next to each name is a location, mostly town or city names.

'I guess the closest is this one called Bruce.' Her finger rests on the map. 'Bruce Lane, believe it or not. It is only a little ways along the coast, a little village called *Shore-sea*.'

'It should only take a couple of hours to get there,' Linn says thoughtfully after passing a road sign. Trying to ignore the sound of her mobile phone ringing again.

'That's really annoying,' Lucy says, trying to get herself comfortable in the car seat. The thing has been going nonstop since they got in the car.

'Could you grab it, it's on the back seat, just switch it off,' Linn says, trying to concentrate on the road.

Lucy leans over and digs around for the annoying little thing. She retrieves it and before switching it off gives an unintentional look at the screen.

'Thirty missed calls from 'Mother', and wow, ten from one called Doctor Williams.' Lucy switches the phone off and then a thought hits her. 'Shit,' she says.

'What?'

'We had group therapy today,' Lucy says then laughs. 'Thank goodness we dodged that bullet.'

Linn giggles. 'It must be why he is calling me.'

After a short silence a thought occurs to her.

'How are we going to find this Bruce guy anyway? There must be loads of them.'

'Only three Bruce Lanes in the whole village,' Lucy replies, staring at her own phone. 'According to the local telephone directory anyhow.'

A stop at the roadside services to stretch their legs, turns into a 'shop till you drop' spending spree of anything that is even nearly edible, and one loaded back seat later they are on the road again. They watch the afternoon passing in a sugar-induced swirling and spiralling maze of tarmac, painted lines, twisting streets, street signs and the occasional blur of something interesting through the window.

Before they know it they are sitting in silence staring out the windscreen of a parked car. Their eyes fixated on two little metal numbers fixed precariously to an old rusty garden gate, which in itself seems to only be held up by the memories of the neglected and abandoned house behind it.

'Are you sure this is the right place?' Linn

asks, sneaking something far too sweet into her mouth.

'What are we even doing anyway?' she adds as an afterthought.

'Yes, this is the place listed in the telephone directory,' Lucy replies, checking her phone again, just to be certain.

'Well, it sure doesn't look like anybody lives there.'

'The neighbours are home,' Lucy says as she squints out the window. The daylight is almost gone and a hazy dusk already settling in the air.

'The neighbours?'

Linn thinks for a moment then grabs an envelope out of her glove box. Before Lucy can get a word in, the car door clicks closed and she can only watch Linn cross the road and knock on the neighbour's front door. A short conversation and a few awkward friendly smiles later, Linn and her ominous white envelope are back in the car.

'Bruce Lane died eight months ago, he was ninety-four years old, no family or friends, and the neighbours wish the council would do something about the property.' Linn exhales.

'You get all that by holding an envelope in your hands?'

Twenty minutes later they find themselves staring at a different sort of property on the other side of the village. A slightly more modern terraced place, crammed into the centre of the old town, for those who love the hub but also enjoy the village life. Row upon row built like it in every town, a place for yuppies, hipsters, and small families all trying to get somewhere other than where they are. Row upon row of lights twinkling out of bay windows, all except one.

'Seems nobody is home.' Linn winds her seat down as far as it will go and leans back with a yawn.

'What are you doing?' Lucy chuckles.

'I have been driving all day, I need a rest.'

And with that Linn promptly closes her eyes and a moment later starts snoring softly to herself. Lucy rolls her eyes back, and fishes out a cigarette.

'I guess we are officially on a stakeout,' she grins to herself.

A couple of hours later the excitement has worn off and turned itself into boredom. There has been no activity around the little terraced apartment, nothing but a growing taste of stale tobacco in Lucy's mouth alongside a growing plethora of empty junk food wrappers around her.

'How long have we been here?' A hazy Linn starts stirring awake.

'God, I feel sick,' Lucy mumbles as she brushes crumbs off her shirt. 'This isn't as fun as it looks in the movies.'

Linn looks at Lucy, and then at the mess of

wrappers already strewn around her little car. She is about to say that she is 'bloody well not surprised,' but then she begins to gag.

'Have you been smoking in...' she starts to ask before something makes her stop mid-sentence. A small movement on the dark street ahead.

Lucy follows her gaze and sees a figure slowly ambling down the dimly lit street, a slight stagger in his step as he appears under one light and then the next. Most likely on his way home from the local.

'Is this our lucky winner?' Lucy says, sounding like a sleuth from an old black and white television show. She has been watching pedestrians pass all night and none were the proud owners of their interesting address.

'God, what time is it?' Linn yawns, her body beginning to surge with aches from the little car seat. It was still light when they arrived.

'Shhhh...' Lucy hisses and seems to grow as tense as a cornered snake.

They watch the figure on the street sway at the bottom of the stairs they were keeping an eye on. Lucy feels like her heart is going to go full drum and bass on her while Linn can suddenly oddly feel the hair growing in her ears.

They both hold their breath and watch the figure teeter one step at a time to the door. He fumbles around with the keys and frustratingly drops them on the pavement. After hovering his hand above them for a minute he fishes them back up, almost falling over in the process, and is back at the keyhole with them. He doesn't see the shadow of Lucy standing behind him. He finally clicks the lock open and begins to retire into the dark hallway. He flicks a light on, then starts as he hears something behind him.

'Mr Bruce Lane?' Lucy asks.

'Sure,' he slurs lasciviously, his drunken thoughts swimming dreamily at the sudden sight of a tall, beautiful, and busty woman at his door.

Lucy watches his eyes undress her and then cracks one of her fists into his face. The sudden solid punch gives a satisfying cracking sound of cartilage breaking and throws him violently to the floor with a torrent of blood gushing out of his broken nose.

'What the hell are you doing?' Linn shrieks from behind Lucy, unable to believe her own eyes.

Lucy ignores her and leans in over the bleeding Bruce.

'I believe you like raping little girls, Mr Bruce Lane,' she sneers down at him. Her mouth is curled into a snarl that's looking for any excuse to tear him apart.

'What?' His eyes shoot open like a couple of tiny fried eggs. 'I...I...didn't...rape anybody,' he stutters and grunts the words out. He can see Lucy is getting ready to punch him again and starts welling up with tears. Almost paralysed with fear he starts desperately slowly shuffling away from her, too petrified to take his eyes off her for even a second.

'Please,' he pleads, his words now thick with blood and tears. 'I don't have much money.' He digs a wallet out and throws it on the floor, his hands shaking with terror. 'Just take it, please, just leave me alone.'

'I don't want your stinking money.' Lucy leans in over him and gets her fist ready for round two.

'Please, no, please,' he begs, openly crying and cowering away from her like an abused puppy.

She looks down at him in disbelief as she watches a dark wet patch start to spread on his trousers before slowly streaming onto the floor next to him into a small puddle.

'No,' she says, and backs away slowly almost in disgust. 'You are too weak to hurt anybody.'

She spins around, pushes past Linn and lights a cigarette. She works her way back to the car looking like a boiling kettle trying its best to simmer down. Linn looks back at the doorway and carnage inside. She cautiously goes inside and looks down at their suspect. He looks pathetic just whimpering there in fear. Lucy is right, it couldn't possibly be him.

'You are going to be fine,' she reassures him as she studies his face. 'Your nose is broken.'

She gently cups his face in her hands to soothe him and with a sudden motion grabs his nose with both hands and painfully realigns it.

He screams.

Linn closes the door behind her, and works her way slowly down the stairs and across the street. Somewhere a dog is barking having heard the noise, but apart from that there are no curtains twitching, none of the neighbours seem interested. Linn sighs, takes a deep breath and sits back in the car next to Lucy. She clenches the steering wheel as tight as possible to stay her anger. She can feel her nails digging into the leather.

'It's not him,' Lucy says slowly.

'What is wrong with you?' Linn seethes. 'How do you even get like this?'

'Like what?'

'Like this.' Linn gestures vaguely around her.

Lucy cocks an eyebrow at Linn then regards her for a short while. 'You can either let life tear you apart or you can get tough, it's that simple.'

'Well the next one we are doing my way,' Linn says, and starts the car, quietly pulls it onto the street and steals them away into the night.

Chapter Ten

a good day

'How long has it been?' Ria asks weakly.

'Must be over a week already, I guess.' Clio answers, unable to calculate how many days they have held captive for with any certainty. Not with all the beatings she receives, sometimes she could have lost a day altogether. She will be defiant till the bitter end, and it seems that day is creeping up on her.

They have somehow gotten used to the routine. Every other day he leaves the farm for most of the day and night. On those days when he does return he is always drunk. That's when he comes visiting them. The visits always end in pain for Clio.

She seems to drift in and out of consciousness like a cloudy sky. Unable to tell if all the little conversations she has with her sister are just dreams. Sometimes she wakes and she is alone in their little cage. Talking to herself in the darkness, listening to the voices echoing back at her. So many voices at first whispering and then screaming at her from the shadows. Sometimes she screams back at them, but no sound comes out of her mouth.

The next morning they get some food

thrown into their cage and wake with him licking his lips while looking down at them.

'You better eat all your food because it's all you're getting today,' he says and then locks the paddock door.

He would have told them not to be stupid and try anything, but he thinks they are getting the message. The one sister, he thinks they are sisters, she really puts up a fight, he had to teach her a lesson. At least he hasn't been stupid enough to hurt the pretty one. He salivates thinking about her as he packs his truck up and gets ready to go, almost sorry to leave.

They had tried to escape once before, so now he has them in a cage. He grins to himself as he drives up the track away from the farm. That's the night he taught that bitch a proper lesson. She is almost broken now, it is a pity, she wasn't that ugly when he had grabbed them, if only she hadn't been so stubborn. He grins to himself again; he kinda enjoyed it though. He rolls the window down, turns the radio up and enjoys the wind in his hair. He has things to do today. He can go back and play later.

'It is looking like a good day here in the Home Counties,' the radio says.

'It sure is, Mr Radio,' he replies.

He has a small office that one of the village locals runs for him. An ugly old slag of a woman, but she is good with the books and knows about farms so he tolerates her. If she hadn't worked for his family so long he would have got himself something better to look at. He grins at her crappy excuse for a smile, thinking he has horses with better looking teeth.

'Good morning, Mavis,' he says as he hangs up his jacket. He won't be staying long but it seems like the thing to do. At least she makes a good cup of tea.

'I will put the kettle on,' she trills in that annoyingly happy way she likes to talk. And boy, does this old goat love to talk. He sits down at his desk and gets ready for her bombardment.

She brings a steaming brew into his little office along with a nice fat wad of work for him.

'These are all the new orders,' she begins, handing him a few folders. 'Your letters,' she says handing him another few folders.

'Just put it all on the desk,' he cuts her off. Sometimes he will just let her ramble on and imagine all the ways he would love to just kill her. He doesn't want to do that today. Today is a good day, it's a Tuesday, it's the day he and a couple of friends get a taxi to the nearest city and enjoy a good old-fashioned strip show and some good sniff up the old nose. He likes Tuesdays.

'Thank you for the tea, Mavis,' he drawls as she leaves.

'Oh that reminds me.' Mavis stops and turns.

'What is it now, Mavis?' he asks and looks

impatiently at his watch.

'A very pretty young lady was here to see you this morning, ever so early. She was literally waiting for me by the door to open the office.'

'A very pretty young lady is it, Mavis? And what did this wee lass want?'

'She said she was a representative of some big company or other, I can't remember the name now for the life of me, but she was ever so polite. Said she could try arrange a meeting with you tomorrow if you like, it's all there in your diary, said her name was Lucy or something.'

Well, today really is looking up for Brucie Boy. A couple of girls back home, a boys' night out, and a pretty young rep to ogle over tomorrow. He downs his tea and tries to get his head around some of the paperwork but just can't get into it. He picks up his landline and dials a number.

'Oi, mate, Bruce here, what you say we get this party started a couple hours early, yeah? Alright, mate, see you in the pub in an hour.'

And faster than you can say *'See you tomorrow, Mavis,'* he is out of the office and headed to the nearest pub.

Unfortunately it's one of the good old taps that have been turned into some new sort of hipster malarkey selling craft ales, but it's the closest one to the office and nice and quiet in the afternoons, and at least the place pulls better birds than it used to.

'Usual please, mate,' he says to the barman, and is contemplating wasting a little time on one of the fruit machines when his day seems to get a whole lot better. He watches the cutest little thing in a miniskirt enter the pub, look around a little lost, and sit awkwardly down at the end of the bar.

Well, well, well, he thinks to himself as he turns around to face his drink and the pretty skirt, suddenly not feeling much in the mood for a slot machine.

A couple of pints later the little sparrow in the skirt is looking a little more lost, she keeps looking around as though she is expecting somebody. Bruce has a shot of the old Dutch courage, and slides along the bar counter towards her.

'Boyfriend late?' he asks, giving her a big old friendly smile.

She seems to blush and fluster a little.

'Me, oh, sorry I am meant to meet a blind date, it's so silly, I am a little late, your name isn't Terrence is it by any chance?' she asks. She really is blushing like a little red rose now. All ready for the plucking.

Bruce laughs; today really just keeps getting better and better.

'No,' he grins back at her. 'My name is Bruce, and what is your name?'

'Linn,' she says with a little smile.

There is something about that smile that didn't sit right with Bruce, but if he plays his cards right tonight he could have three little birds in his cage.

The smile he returns to Linn sends a cold shiver down her spine.

Chapter Eleven

drugs kill

Lucy has hardly slept since this little road trip started, she is running on caffeine, chocolate and tobacco. Along with a few cheeky drinks here and there she keeps herself floating. Besides, staring out the windscreen is like a night at the drive-in. *God, do those things even exist anymore?* A real live action starring the one and only Linn, and introducing our villain, Mr Bruce Lane the pervert.

She chuckles and lights her little joint again; hell, she may have a little fun. She stares back out the windscreen again into the pub window across the street. It really is like a cinema, she has a front row seat on the two of them.

'Look at me, I am a vulnerable young lady,' she says, trying to mimic Linn.

'And I am a big bad wolf,' she mimics Bruce talking, trying to sound as husky as she can. She chokes, takes another hit of the joint and throws it out the window.

'My, what big teeth you have,' she carries on, mimicking Linn.

'All the better to eat you with, ha ha ha ha,' she chortles quietly to herself, the game not seeming so funny anymore.

She grabs another plastic bag of crap food

and starts thinking she should have got some popcorn for this feature presentation. She's so stoned and has the munchies so bad that she can swear she even smells popcorn, and it smells so damn good.

The whole scene reminds her of one of those dating shows, she hates those things, but this is actually kinda funny, she is beginning to see the appeal. Lucy has never been a girly girl, she hates soap operas and fucking hairdos, goddamned make-up, manicures and pedicures, she even hates high heels. Fuck all that shit. She had seemed to always be a rocket headed in this direction, but not little Miss Linn over there, the guest star of tonight's show.

She is quite the fire-cracker though, little Miss PhD pulled out a bag full of medical stuff, and a whole bunch of different drugs. Lucy is not that much into anything more than a beer and a joint, harmless shit really. She doesn't know what half the stuff in that bag of Linn's is, nor does she want to. Drugs kill, man, a yellow brick road of illusion. She can barely even pronounce the crap written on those bottles. She has been fists up with some strong people in her life, but none of them scare Lucy as much as that bag of drugs next to her does.

Inside the bar it seems big bad Bruce has a few friends joining the party. He has a word in one of their ears and they saunter out the pub and into a cab on their own, leaving the young lovers to it. Lucy clenches her fist.

'Come on, Linn, this is your chance, do it,' she chants softly to herself. Her heart is floundering all over the place, she is literally on the edge of her seat, transfixed on the thriller playing out right before her eyes. Every now and then she has to remind herself to breathe.

'Do it,' she repeats.

She watches Linn making her excuses and leave to 'powder her nose' as women do.

This is it, Lucy thinks to herself, and leans forward in her seat.

Bruce seems to look about him all innocent enough, pull something out a pocket and then hovers over Linn's drink like a damned vulture. He scans around him again quickly and then...

'Bingo!' Lucy shrieks and then sinks down into her seat again, trying not to draw attention to herself. He bloody well did it, he roofied her drink. This shit is about to get real.

Linn stares at herself in the mirror. The barbiturates she took to calm her nerves don't seem to be helping much, she is shaking like a leaf on the inside. Every instinct in her is telling her to run.

Run away, Linn. Run, Linn, run.

She stares at her trembling face in the mirror, clutching the sink as though her very life depends on it. A myriad of faces swirl around her reflection like ghosts trapped behind a cracked dirty window.

'You have to be tough,' Lucy says.

'You cannot run from everything in life,' Dr Williams says.

'You are one of us now,' Jack says.

'Why won't you just speak to me?' her mother says.

Linn sobs and looks down at the sink, watching her own little tears hitting the porcelain. She wants to scream her head off, just scream until it all goes away. She scrambles around in her bag for some more of those tranquillisers, and pops a couple more of them down her throat. She then pulls out a pint of milk and downs it. It will line her stomach and throat for what's about to happen. She digs a syringe out of her bag and preps it, then pockets it for the right moment. She breathes in and out for a few moments, then finds her wind and gets ready to leave the little toilet.

Everything seems to be going in slow motion. She can feel literally every beat her heart makes. *God, have I taken too many of those pills?* She thinks to herself. *Drunk too much? I really ought not to be mixing the two.*

Her nerves hit her stomach like a tightening fist in the guts and she scampers back into one of the cubicles. She remembers a boyfriend at uni that used to be in a band, before each gig his stomach would tie up into knots, and he would

get the runs each and every time. The simple fix
was anti-diarrhoea tablets, she feels like kicking
herself for not thinking of it. She checks her bag
again and makes sure the syringe is ready. She
also pulls a small pill out and puts it in her
pocket. She closes her eyes and whispers a small
prayer. It is then that she really gets the urge to
just call her mother, tell her that she loves her.
She just sits there staring at the phone shaking
in her nervous hand until the urge subsides.

When she makes it back to the bar Bruce is
all bright smiles and eyes. If it was not for the
circumstances, he might seem quite charming in
an awkward sort of way. But there is something
dark and maniacal behind that mask he calls a
face, she just can't see it yet. She sips her drink
slowly.

'Oh my,' she feigns disbelief at the watch on
her wrist. 'How long have we been talking?' She
also forces a smile that feels more like a grimace.

'Time flies when you having fun, doesn't it.'
He grins at her.

'Have you been having fun, Bruce?' she
blinks and slurs the words out, pretending to be
a little more inebriated than she really is.

Bruce gives her another devilish grin.

'You look like a bad boy, are you a bad boy,
Bruce?' She drawls his name out long and slow
as she traces a flirtatious finger along the

contours of his face.

Don't fuck it up, Linn.

She doesn't give him a chance to answer.

'Tell you what, big boy, let me get us a drink for the road and you can walk me to the train.'

'Sure,' he chuckles, but she has already put her drink down and sauntered off to find the barman.

When she arrives back she is cradling two shots in her hands, hoping nobody saw her drop anything in one of the glasses. She hands him one with a nervous smile, and holds hers up ready.

'I am so glad I met you today,' she says.

'Me too,' he replies as they chink the two glasses together and down the strong liqueur.

Linn then downs her remaining drink and drags him out of the bar pretending to not want to miss her train, but the reality is that the game is afoot and now every single minute counts.

They have not even made it a block away before big strong Bruce starts staggering and swaying.

'I don't feel well,' he strains to say, even standing is becoming difficult for him. He is crouched over as though he is going to hurl, then a sudden horrible realisation occurs to him.

'What have you done?' He groans, and looks up at Linn but she isn't next to him. Before he can turn around he feels a horrible stabbing pain tear through him, then he sees Linn behind him holding something in her hand. A long sinister needle glistening in the darkness.

'What is that?' he asks and tries to reach for her, but his legs don't seem to be listening anymore, and he falls over like an old overfilled sack.

It is kind of beautiful, like flying, he thinks as he hits the ground. He stares at the stars in the night sky above him, then his view is broken by a woman's face looking down at him.

'You aren't Linn,' he giggles.

He turns his head to the side and sees Linn crouched over with a finger down her throat trying to make herself get sick. He looks back up at the face above him.

Lucy glares down at him then puckers her lips and drops a wad of spit down on his face. She grins admiringly at her handiwork and then stomps down on him hard.

'Sweet dreams,' she sneers, and then the stars are all gone and there is just darkness.

He can hear the two women talking in the distance far away, can feel hands sliding him somewhere, then picking him up. He feels as light as a feather. The last thing he can hear is a car engine start, and then nothing, not even the pinprick of a single dream in the thick darkness.

Chapter Twelve

the high road

Linn feels like somebody left a jack-hammer running loose in her head, and her mouth is drier than an old bit of cardboard. When she opens her eyes, the sudden sunlight drowning her eyes with painful brightness slowly fades as she blinks to get some moisture back into them, and her eyelids rasp against her eyeballs like jagged sandpaper.

She is sitting in a car seat. She looks out the window and sees a parking lot around her. On the other side is a small green and some picnic tables. Lucy is out there sitting on one of those tables, smoking a cigarette. She sees Linn staring out and with a little wave she grins back at her.

Linn looks down at her arm; she seems to have had the sense to put a drip in before she passed out. A bit of Flumazenil to counteract any drugs still in her system. She doesn't even remember doing it. She pulls out the needle and ambles out of the car towards Lucy. Her body aches and groans in complaint, but that big old grin on Lucy's face seems to draw her in.

Lucy gets up and gives Linn a big solid

embrace.

'How are you feeling?' She beams proudly at Linn.

'Absolutely bloody awful,' Linn confesses.

Lucy grins and hands her a cold bottle of water that feels like heaven on Linn's raspy throat. And then the two of them sit awhile staring back at the car.

'Is he…'

'Still passed out in the boot,' Lucy smiles and nods.

'How long?'

'I have been driving around all night waiting for you to wake up.'

Linn looks down at her watch. Six in the morning already.

'I got some sandwiches too,' Lucy smiles and pushes a little bag of goodies toward Linn. 'Food will probably do you some good after your hot date last night.' Lucy snickers.

The two of them sit there a little while longer chewing in reflective silence before Linn studies Lucy a little.

'You know, I never asked much about your life,' Linn muses.

Lucy stares back at her thoughtfully, chewing a bit too much on her mouthful.

'I tried become a cop once,' she says, savouring the surprise on Linn's face. 'They said I was too violent,' she adds for dessert, and the two of them can't help but chuckle together at the thought. The laughter subsides when they both hear banging and shouting coming from the car. They look at one another and race back over there.

The two of them stare at the boot not knowing quite what to do. It is obvious that Bruce is awake, and not very keen on being shut in a car.

'So what now?' Lucy asks as the car begins shaking around as though it is prom night.

'We need to get him talking,' Linn says.

'Let's drive out somewhere quiet, I will get him talking.'

'You know I love your enthusiasm, Lucy, but we agreed to do this my way.'

'So, then, what now?'

'You need to hold him down for me,' Linn says while frantically trying to dig her bag out of the car.

Lucy watches Linn get one of her special syringes ready then searches in her jeans pocket and pulls out little Miss Daisy. Now, she may only be a set of brass knuckles, but little Miss Daisy has saved Lucy's life more than once. She got that name because the finger holes reminded Lucy of a daisy, of all things.

Linn watches Lucy slide the brass knuckles onto her fingers, and before she even gets a chance to say anything she is watching Lucy kick the boot door open and start punching the hell out of Bruce. Even being the brute he is, he doesn't stand a chance against Lucy in his condition. It is all over in less than a minute. He gets a good kick in on Lucy's face before she almost cracks his skull into pieces, putting him back to sleep herself. She doesn't even have to hold him down for Linn to inject him.

'We need him on the back seat for this,' Linn says, a little shaken and horrified by the sudden violence and Bruce's bloody face.

Lucy sucks deep on her cigarette with a shaking hand that is still streaked with the thin lines of recent blood. 'Fine,' she says and exhales.

When Bruce next wakes up his whole world has changed. It had gone from a very good day to a very strange day, very quickly. His mind is all messed up like he has cotton wool in it. He can barely see anything, he thinks he is driving somewhere, he is with two pretty girls, he knows he must be really messed up on drugs or dreaming, or something, but he doesn't care, he feels good, he thinks he does, he can't quite remember. He looks out the car window and sees a unicorn running next to the car, then it grows wings and flies away.

Linn slaps him.

'Tell us about your other girls,' she says and licks his face. She has a long reptilian tongue that doesn't seem to end, and when it finally does end, the tongue is forked like a snakes. She swallows her tongue and giggles, then seems to disappear into the mist somewhere, but he can still hear both of them laughing somewhere in the distance.

He dreams he is in bed with both of them, the same dream he has about the two sisters at the farm.

'Where is the farm?' he hears one of the girls say; the other one is still giggling.

'I am not meant to tell anybody,' he says, unsure.

'We can have so much fun together, all five of us.'

He smiles as he sees the four girls swimming around him. They draw him in and seduce him with their siren song.

'Yes,' he says lost in his dream. 'So much fun together, let's go to my farm.'

'Where is the farm?' they giggle.

He tells them.

The laughing suddenly stops and the dream ends like a cold hard punch in the nuts.

GLEN MATTHEW SMITH

Chapter Thirteen

the low road

When Bruce stirs awake he is in the back of a car, everything is a blur and he feels like hell. It takes a while for him to slowly come around. His mouth is dry, his body hurts, and there is a ringing in his ears that won't seem to go away. He quickly realises his arms and legs are tied, and in the fog can begin to discern somebody in the front seat. He slowly tilts his head to look out the window and feels a deep hole suddenly drop from inside him. They are at his farm. He watches in horror as somebody outside starts opening the doors in his barn. And then it all slowly starts coming back to him.

Linn looks back at the car. It is a big farm and Lucy is waiting in the car while she checks the some of the outer buildings. She sees Bruce slumped over in the back, his eyes all vacant against the window, and turns her attention back to the barn. There is something wrong about the path into the barn, something familiar about it.

Then it hits her. It is the same path from her nightmares. She walks towards the barn and seems to be back in those nightmares. It all starts to swim around her, and she can feel herself trembling in fear, but she pushes on, she has to.

She reaches out, the whole world shaking and trembling around her just as much as she is inside. She opens the door with Bruce's keys.

She does not know how she knew which door to open, there are so many in the barn. It all seems just like her nightmares, the muddy path, the door in front of her. She can almost hear Dr Williams telling her to open the door. But when she does open the door the similarities end. There is no chair, nobody looking like her tied to it. What there is, however, is a cage, and inside that cage are two women looking as scared as hell. Linn's heart explodes with emotion. She was right all along. Jack had been right.

'It's okay, I am one of you,' she says, wiping away a tear.

Bruce waits for his moment to act; he doesn't know who these bitches are, what they did to him, but this shit is ending here. He kinda thinks he recognises that one poking around in his barn. Everything is wrong, how does she have his keys, know which door to open? Who even is this bitch in the front seat? She is a dead bitch, that's who she is.

Bruce gets his second wind and strangles the ties that are holding his arms together around the woman in the front seat.

He leans all his weight back against her throat and the head rest. He is a fat bastard and it is easy work. He doesn't care what the story is, who is she is, what her fucking name is, this is his farm.

Lucy is pinned down, choking it out, unable to do anything but slowly stop struggling against the chord around her neck.

How ironic, she thinks, as the darkness slowly takes her; she had tied them herself, she knows she can't break the ropes and knots sucking her life out of her, all she can do is choke and wheeze. It is not long before she is out cold and Bruce is staggering away from the car toward the barn.

Linn is fumbling between Bruce's keys trying to open the cage and let the two girls out when she feels the hairs on her back all stand up as though she is a cat. She slowly turns around and sees Bruce grinning down at her. Her heart turns ice cold. She watches his fist fly through the air. Feels it hit her like a rock. She feels herself flying through the air, and when she hits the ground she thinks how beautiful it is that dust rises so slowly when you fall in the dirt.

When Linn wakes up again she is being dragged in the dirt by Bruce. He is muttering something to himself. He has her by the foot and her head is grazing the ground painfully. She must be slightly concussed because she kinda doesn't care anymore, doesn't feel anything anymore. Everything is upside down. She knows she is going to die this time, and she doesn't care because for the first time in a long time she is at peace. It all makes sense now, the nightmares, the list, Jack, the others. She laughs.

Bruce stops dragging her, drops her leg, and looks down at her.

'I am going to burn you, bitch, burn you alive,' he sneers down at her.

But Linn just starts laughing more.

He wants to tell her to stop screaming because nobody is going to hear it, but she isn't screaming, she isn't even scared. She is ruining everything, all his fun by just laughing madly and looking over there.

Bruce follows Linn's eyes and an axe swishes past his face. He glares down at Ria. He remembers the little bitch had the keys in the lock when he had grabbed her and...

Clio comes screaming in like a mad banshee from hell and jumps onto him, wrapping herself around his shoulders, and starts trying to choke him. She is too frail and weak to do much more than hang on to him and try her best.

Bruce leans down over Linn and grabs her by the throat, throttling her little head until it turns into a bright red tomato. She caused all this. Clio is doing little more than making this more fun. They tell him not to have fun with the girls. Today Bruce is having his fun. He feels himself getting excited then the axe smacks painfully into his side.

He turns to see a fat grin from Ria's wild face. He snickers back at her when she realises she has hit him with the wrong end of the axe. He punches her bad. Out cold. He will show them all who is boss.

He throws Clio off him, crashing her against a tree, then he gets to work on Linn again. He kicks her, punches her stupid face till its' nice and bloody, then the stupid thing starts laughing again, laughing mad, this mad little woman really is freaking him out. He looks up and sees Lucy in all her beautifully dark glory, her whole life spent seething for this moment.

'You should have made sure I was dead,' Lucy says, soothing her bruised neck, a twisted sneer on her face. She is ready for this fight.

Lucy punches him with Miss Daisy in the kisser. It is a rewarding crunchy sound of breaking teeth.

He staggers back. Blood gushing out his mouth.

The idiot then tries to charge her. She remembers her training and easily sidesteps him. Watching him topple haplessly to the ground.

He is up in an adrenaline fuelled heartbeat, and tries to charge her again but Miss Daisy stops him dead in his tracks, and again he kisses the dirt.

'Not so easy now, is it?' Lucy chuckles.

Ria, being somewhat more conscious, seizes her opportunity, pounces at her axe on the ground, and without a single hesitation she screams and buries the axe deep into his face. A face she has grown to hate more than anything. She keeps searing the axe into it until it becomes unrecognisable. Lucy stops her, pulls her in close and gives Ria a big hug. And with that, a bloody axe and a dead corpse drop to the ground.

Linn finds her wind, and slowly crawls over to the unmoving body against the tree. She does not know these girls, but she is going to try her best to help them, all of them. She crawls painfully towards Clio. Lucy and the other girl are in tears, a dead and bloody Bruce at their feet.

'Hey,' Linn says, cradling Clio's head.

She taps Clio's face softly.

'Hey,' Linn says.

Clio blinks.

'Hi,' she says.

'My name is Linn.'

'Hey, Linn, you don't have any chocolate, do you? I miss chocolate so much.'

'Sure I do,' Linn sniffs, trying not try cry as she looks over at Lucy and sees Lucy looking straight back at her, still holding a distraught

Ria in her arms. Lucy and Linn give each other
a small tear-soaked smile.

GLEN MATTHEW SMITH

Epilogue

jack and the fox

You can't escape your nightmares, they are there with you, even when you are awake.

Jack sits staring at the pond. There is nothing exceptional about it, but it is the most even mildly interesting thing on the whole clinic grounds, apart from the cliffs, and most patients aren't allowed on the cliffs.

Six months of this crap, he has lost his hair, his will to live, and the only thing keeping him together are his daily talks with Gilbert here at the pond. And yet, today of all days Gilbert doesn't show.

Jack throws a stone at the water and says goodbye to the horrible place.

He asks about Gilbert at the front desk as he is leaving. The nurse in the tight-fitting whites tells him there is no such patient.

Jack describes him.

Then she starts singing a different tune.

'Mr Gilbert died almost a year ago,' she says. 'There is no possible way you could have seen him.'

'Yeah, I have heard it all before, but this is a new one,' Jack says thoughtfully.

Jack takes the quickest cab out of the place.

So when you beat the big C, the big cancerous C that should have been a four-letter word, you don't get a damn medal, you get a new life. As far as Jack cares, he should have died way back when in that cabin. And then a good few times before that too. But here he is, a recovered man talking to ghosts for the past six months. Jack sighs and jumps out the cab at the beach.

He is overdressed but he doesn't care, in fact the sand is so hot, he is glad to be wearing shoes and a shirt as he drifts out of place towards the beach bar. The wind twirls up a sandstorm on the beach behind him.

Joe gives him one of those big cheesy smiles when he gets to the beach bar and slides an empty glass at him. Joe rummages around and digs out a treasured bottle, then slides it over to Jack.

'To keep the glass company, my friend.' Joe smiles and pours two glasses from the bottle for each of them.

'I don't usually drink on the clock but today is a special day.' Joe salutes Jack and downs his drink.

Jack grins and follows suit.

'Sorry about the vixen, nothing to do with me old chap,' Joe says and saunters off.

'Wha...?' is all Jack can say before he sees a familiar face.

A pair of cold beautiful eyes lock on him from across the bar.

'You look good for a dead man, Jack, or is it Frank now?' Misty sings her words at him. A knowing grin sickly cut across her face. He has forgotten how alluring and mysterious she is, as though she is written straight out of an old hard-boiled paperback. She is sipping from one of those cocktails that have an umbrella swimming around in it. As hot as it is, Misty always looks like a cool breeze blown in from a man's imagination.

'Candy was never the type to take many extravagant holidays,' Misty says coolly. 'And then when she starts taking holidays with her girl down to the beach every month, I start getting curious.'

Misty smiles softly and sits next to Jack.

Jack says nothing and takes a long cold sip of something expensive. Joe must have been saving this a long while, it tastes like a special occasion.

'Congratulations on beating cancer, Jack,' Misty smiles and clinks her glass against his.

Joe seizes the opportunity and pours him and Jack another round and gives the biggest smile as he nods and clinks his own glass against theirs. The three of them are silent for a while as they thirstily empty the glasses.

'I take it you finally took the witness relocation option after what happened in that cabin?' Misty puzzles. 'Changed your name, faked your death? Big bad gangsters suddenly scare you, Jack?'

'I don't know if God keeps trying to kill me and failing miserably at it,' Jack reflects as he teases his lips with some more of the good stuff. 'I should have died in that cabin.'

Misty clears her throat.

'The girl that saved you is a damn good nurse,' Misty smiles at him softly. 'It is part of the reason I am here.'

She slides a newspaper over at Jack.

Jack ignores the paper and stares at her.

'Turns out she found a list of names before she fled that cabin, you wouldn't know anything about that would you, Jack?'

Jack just keeps on staring, as cool as a cucumber in one of her umbrella drinks.

'Seems she and her friend found the first name on said list, presumably kill said name and now I believe after rescuing a couple of missing sisters, there are now four girls hunting down the names on that list.'

Jack raises his eyebrows.

'Hmmmm,' Misty coos. 'Quite the hornet's nest you kicked up, isn't it, Jack?'

'I will tell you the kicker, Jack, she showed Nugget the list before her and her friend go AWOL from therapy and become all *Thelma and*

Louise.

This does kick a grin onto Jack's face, a nice big fat one, Nugget will remember every last word on that list, beautiful autistic Nugget.

Misty nods at him, the same smile spreading on to her face now.

'It seems our little nurse also has an estranged brother who is now, as we speak, driving in a car with her therapist, tracking those four girls down with the mobile phone that her mother sent her. God bless rich protective paranoid mothers.' Misty downs another cocktail and Joe mixes her a fresh one.

'Don't worry about the girls, Jack, I am monitoring the situation, but you may want to read the newspaper.' Misty toys a slender finger around her voluptuous moist lips.

Jack knows Misty is the ultimate queen bee, if she says she is watching the girls, they may as well have a guardian angel looking over them. If Jack remembers some of those names on the list, they are going to need all the help they can get; then the front page stops his train of thought dead.

After a tumult of bizarre events that ended with the death of a Member of Parliament, Captain Tommy Warwick, an ex-special forces officer, was arrested for her assassination. The day began with the capital city being shocked by his appearance in a leaked video footage of a suspected terrorist attempt to film his death after being recognised as a previously serving officer in the forces.

Officials have begun a thorough investigation into the series of events along with their possible connection with the foiled terror attack at a train station along the main line earlier on in the afternoon. The suspect had reportedly surrendered himself to authorities after the murder. No formal press release has been issued by the Home Office yet.

Jack sighs and shoves a cigarette in his mouth.

Misty politely removes it from between his lips and coyly breaks it up onto the bar counter. She wrinkles her nose innocently at his exasperated glare.

Jack sighs again.

'He is a good kid.'

'I know,' Misty replies softly.

'All this catching up is quite heartbreaking, Misty, but why are you really here?'

Misty pouts and then swivels playfully around in her stool.

'Let's go for a walk, Jack.'

Jack and Misty brave the windy sand swept beach and seem to fade away into it as they mark a path along the water's edge.

'I gave Candy a couple of weeks off, Jack, I also got you guys a room at the resort.' Misty gives Jack a key, a smile, and a wink.

'Thanks, Misty, for everything,' Jack says. He is still waiting for the big white elephant she is going to drop on him. What dragged her all the way out here.

Sensing his anticipation she clears her throat.

'Jack, do you remember the *Fox*?'

'Sure I do, thanks for taking care of tha...'

'He was my brother,' she purrs sadly.

Jack stops walking. The wind cuts at him with tiny sharp edges of sand. He can't see anything else on the beach apart from Misty and the growing sandstorm around them. Jack is suddenly getting a very bad feeling, even the sky above seems to be growing dark and grey.

'Don't worry, Jack, I am not here to avenge him. I am here to tell you a story.' She smiles weakly and holds her hand out for him.

'What kind of story, Misty?' He can see she is broken already, this conversation difficult for her. For the first time he can recall, Misty is looking a little delicate. A little moist around the eyes. Can he even see a little jitter in her hand? He can't stomach seeing Misty looking vulnerable, it has all types of wrong written all over it, so he takes her hand and the two of them carry on walking arm in arm.

'Just a little story about a fox,' Misty sobs.